Princess Poppy

FANTASTIC, NO PLASTIC!

JANEY LOUISE JONES · JENNIE POH

EDEN COOPER

Princess Poppy and her puppy, Sidney, were on the
train with Grandpa. Daisy was having a beach party!
Grandpa dozed while Poppy read about a competition.

"Love Our Planet Competition!
Create an object which could
replace a plastic one! First
prize – boat trip to see seals!"

Princess Poppy

FANTASTIC, NO PLASTIC!

Dedicated to

Willow Swift

Special thanks to:

Paul Lawston, Environmental Education Consultant

Hugh Dignon, Head of Wildlife and Biodiversity, Scottish Government

EDEN COOPER

First published in Great Britain in 2019 by Eden Cooper

1 3 5 7 9 10 8 6 4 2

Text copyright © Janey Louise Jones, 2020
Illustrations copyright © Jennie Poh, 2020

The moral rights of the author and illustrator have been asserted.

Editorial direction and editing by Stephanie Stahl
Art direction and design by Rachel Lawston

A CIP catalogue record for this book is available from the British Library.

Paperback ISBN 978-1-9164484-2-1

Printed and bound in Great Britain.

The paper and board used in this book are made
from wood from responsible sources.

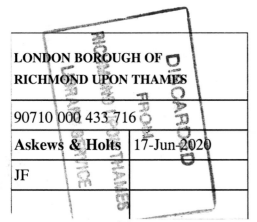

MIX
Paper from
responsible sources
FSC
www.fsc.org FSC® C022174

Eden Cooper
11 Linkfield Road,
Musselburgh, East Lothian,
Edinburgh EH21 7LG

www.edencooper.com

"Wow! This is a great idea!" squealed Poppy.

"Let's think, Sidney. . ." said Poppy,
"what things are made from plastic?"

She made a list on her i-pad.

Sidney wagged his tail. 'Woof!'

PENS
LUNCH BOXES
BAGS
STRAWS
DOLLS
BUBBLE–BATH BOTTLES
TOYS

As Poppy thought, Sidney went quiet. Oh no!
He was eating Poppy's sandwiches.

"Sidney!" she said, looking at the puppy.
"They're not for you!"

Sidney blew a raspberry which made Grandpa laugh. When Poppy told Sidney he'd been naughty, he stuck his tongue out and lay down, looking the other way!

They arrived at Camomile Cove where Daisy and Louie were waiting. Sidney leapt onto the platform.

"Sidney, come back!" called Poppy.
But he just shook his bottom at her!

"Let's go!' said Daisy. 'Before we party, we want to pick up all the plastic on the beach."

"That's so cool!" said Poppy.

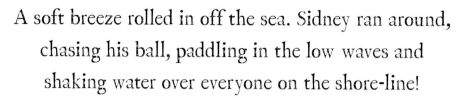

A soft breeze rolled in off the sea. Sidney ran around, chasing his ball, paddling in the low waves and shaking water over everyone on the shore-line!

"Aw, Sidney!" laughed Daisy, after a soaking. "I'm going to catch you! And tickle you!" Daisy started to chase the puppy and he ran away as fast as he could.

"Woof, woof!"

Poppy giggled.

"What a lot of plastic stuff!" said
Louie, looking along the beach.

Scattered on the sand were plastic bottles,
carrier bags, old toys, straws and stirrers,
empty containers and plastic lids.

"I know," agreed Poppy,
"It's terrible for the creatures in the ocean."

Grandpa had a snooze in a deck chair.

Princess Poppy and the others
got busy with the clean-up.

Meanwhile Sidney carried on playing
around on the beach on his own, chasing
seagulls and chewing on sticks. He looked
a bit lonely and was feeling rather bored!

He dug in the sand. . .

He played chase with
other dogs. . .

He sunbathed for a few moments. . .

But then something caught his eye
stuck in between two rocks. . .

It was a green plastic bag, fluttering and flapping in the breeze.

Sidney ran to the bag, sniffed it and started chewing on it.

Louie noticed that the puppy was almost choking.

"Everyone!" he called. "Come quickly! Sidney needs us."

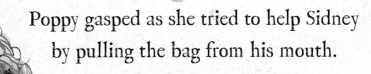

"**Oh no, Sidney!**" cried Poppy,
rushing to rescue her puppy.

Sidney had tried to eat some of the plastic
bag and it was now caught in his throat.

Poppy gasped as she tried to help Sidney
by pulling the bag from his mouth.

He wasn't happy at all.

Grandpa took charge. He managed to get all the
plastic out of Sidney's mouth and throat.

"Daisy darling, can you call Willow, the vet
and ask her to come quickly." he said.

Poor Sidney was **coughing** and **spluttering**. It sounded to Poppy like he was sobbing, which made Poppy sob too.

As Willow, the vet arrived, she checked Sidney's throat.

"Sidney is going to be just fine." said Willow.

"Phew," said Poppy, holding her puppy's paw.

"Lucky you were here," said Willow. "But imagine how the seals, turtles, fish and birds feel, with nobody to remove the plastic they swallow? We need to think of them more!"

"We definitely do," agreed Princess Poppy. She really wanted to win a trip to see seals, but now she truly wanted to help them too. It was time for ACTION!

Poppy wanted to help everyone to use less plastic. But, how?

I must create an object that can easily replace a plastic one! thought Poppy.

What had just happened to little Sidney was terrible.

"There must be ways for people to use less plastic!" she said.

Sidney settled down for a nap with Grandpa, while Poppy and the others had fun at the beach party. They enjoyed the sandcastle competition, the shell necklace making class . . .

The races . . .

The rock-pooling . . .

and finally the picnic!

As they were setting up their picnic, Poppy and Daisy looked back and gasped at the pile of plastic that had been gathered from a tiny stretch of beach.

"Imagine how much of this there is on beaches all over the world!"
said Grandpa.
"And in the sea!"

"It's a mountain of plastic!"
said Daisy.

"No wonder our sea
creatures need our help!"
said Poppy.

"We need to do something about the plastic we waste . . ." said Grandpa. "About half of all the plastic is used only once, then thrown away,"

"Whoa, that's terrible!" said Louie.

"And 90% of all rubbish in our oceans is plastic," Grandpa explained.

"So, we have to use less plastic. ALL of us!" said Daisy.

"**Absolutely,**" said Grandpa. "One **big** problem is plastic can take **hundreds of years** to break down."

"So it just swishes about in the ocean and washes up on our beaches?" said Poppy.

Grandpa nodded.

After the picnic, they took all the bags full of plastic to the recycling point on the promenade.

RECYCLING

Back in Honeypot Hill that night, Poppy went back to her list of plastic objects for the competition. She wrote down some good non-plastic versions of everyday things . . .

Pens
try wooden pencils and pens

Lunch box
use beeswax wrap, reusable
box and thermos

Bags
always use cloth bags

Straws
don't need these at all
or use paper straws

Bubble-bath bottles
glass can be recycled

Toys
wooden

As Poppy tucked Sidney into his bed for the night, she thought about all the creatures in the sea affected by plastics.

Fish

Sea turtles

Birds

Seals and sea lions

Whales and dolphins

Princess Poppy wanted to do something to help out all these animals . . .

After what happened to Sidney today,
she'd never want to use
a plastic bag again!

"I know!" Poppy cried,
"I will ask Mum to help me make
a re-usable bag for shopping!"

Next day, Princess Poppy and Mum made a lovely
colourful shopping bag from old curtains!

"Oh, I love it!" Poppy smiled. "Mum, you know what would be great," she said.
"If we could make lots of bags and sell them to collect money for helping animals
hurt by plastic! This could be my idea for the Love Our Planet competition!"

"BRILLIANT IDEA!" said Mum proudly.

Princess Poppy sent her bag design idea to the competition.

"Even though Honeypot Hill is a little village, we can still make a BIG difference on plastics," said Poppy.

"Definitely," agreed Mum. "We don't want any more plastic polluting our beautiful oceans. And these bags will really help."

Poppy was overjoyed when she won the competition!

Mum went with her on the marvellous boat ride. Poppy dressed as
a mermaid! And Sidney went too! They saw lots of seals!

Poppy had her picnic in her new
cloth bag. But Sidney still got into the
sandwiches first! But with beeswax wraps,
there was nothing to worry about!

"Fantastic! No more plastic!" said Poppy.

GRANDPA'S PLASTIC FACTS

PLASTIC BREAK DOWN TIMES:

- Plastic Bottle – 450 years
- Foamed Plastic Cup – 50 years
- Plastic Straw – 200 years
- Plastic Bag – 20 years

Although the plastic breaks down, it usually breaks down into smaller and smaller bits of plastic – microplastics. These are then consumed by animals and humans

EVERY WEEK a human will accidentally eat the equivalent of one credit card's worth of microplastic

BY 2050 there could be as much plastic in the ocean by weight as there are fish

A TRUCKLOAD OF PLASTIC enters the ocean every minute and UK supermarkets produce 800,000 tonnes of plastic every year

500 BILLION PLASTIC BAGS are used per year! Only 1 in 20 are recycled

OVER THE LAST TEN YEARS we produced more plastic than in the whole of the previous 100

RECYCLING

HOW TO BE PLASTIC FREE

Use cloth bags for your shopping and metal or glass reusable bottles for your drinks

Reduce everyday plastics such as sandwich bags and juice cartons by replacing them with a reusable lunch bag/ box that includes a thermos and beeswax food wraps

Go digital! No need for plastic cds, dvds and cases when you can buy your music and videos online

Volunteer at a beach clean-up

Support plastic bag bans

Spread the word. Talk to your family and friends about why it is important to reduce plastic in our lives and the terrible impacts of plastic pollution

JOIN THE FUN! CAN YOU HELP ME FIND THESE CREATURES AND PLASTIC INSIDE MY STORYBOOK?

Spot these 4 creatures on the beach.

Search for these 4 creatures in the sea and rock pools.

Now find these 4 pieces of plastic rubbish.

 Puffin

 Dolphin

 Plastic Bag

 Gull

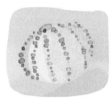 Sea Urchin

 Plastic Straw

 Oyster Catcher

 Sea Anemone

 Plastic Bottle

 Crab

 Seal

 Plastic packaging